For Sandrine

Text copyright © 2009 by NorthSouth Books Inc., New York 10016.
Illustrations copyright © 2007 by Quentin Gréban.
First published in Belgium by Mijade, 16-18, rue de l'Ouvrage B-5000 Namur, under the title *Blanche-Neige*.
All rights reserved.
No part of this book may be reproduced or utilized in any form or by any means, electronic or mechanical,
including photo-copying, recording, or any information storage and retrieval system, without permission
in writing from the publisher.

First published in the United States, Great Britain, Canada, Australia, and New Zealand in 2009
by NorthSouth Books Inc., an imprint of NordSüd Verlag AG, CH-8005 Zürich, Switzerland.
First paperback edition published in the United States, Great Britain, Canada, Australia, and New Zealand in 2013
by NorthSouth Books Inc., an imprint of NordSüd Verlag AG, CH-8005 Zürich, Switzerland.
Distributed in the United States by NorthSouth Books Inc., New York 10016.
Typography by Christy Hale

Library of Congress Cataloging-in-Publication Data is available.
ISBN: 978-0-7358-2257-3 (trade edition).
10 9 8 7 6 5 4 3 2 1
ISBN: 978-0-7358-4116-1 (paperback edition).
10 9 8 7 6 5 4 3 2 1
Printed in China by Leo Paper Products Ltd., Heshan, Guangdong, January 2013

www.northsouth.com

MIX
Paper from
responsible sources
FSC® C020056

The Brothers Grimm

Snow White

illustrated by Quentin Gréban

North
South

One winter day, as snow fell like feathers from the sky, a good queen sat at her window embroidering. Suddenly she pricked her finger, and three drops of blood fell upon the snow.

"Oh," she said, sighing, "if only I had a child with skin as white as snow, lips as red as blood, and hair as black as this ebony embroidery frame, then I would be happy."

Time passed, and the queen had a daughter who was all she had hoped for. She named her child Snow White. But soon after the girl was born, the good queen died.

After a year had passed, the king took another wife. The new queen was beautiful, but she did not love Snow White. All the queen cared about was her own beauty. This queen had a magic mirror, and every day she stood before it and asked,

> "Looking glass upon the wall,
> Who is fairest of us all?"

And the mirror would answer,

> "You are fairest of them all."

As the years passed, Snow White grew lovelier and lovelier, and one day when the queen went to her mirror, the mirror answered,

> "Queen, you are full fair, 'tis true,
> But Snow White is more fair than you."

The queen was furious, and envy filled her heart. She called for a huntsman and told him, "Take the child into the woods and kill her—and bring me her heart to show that you have done it."

The huntsman obeyed and took Snow White into the woods.

But when he drew his knife to kill her, Snow White wept. "Please, dear huntsman, do not take my life. Leave me in the woods, and I will never come home again."

The huntsman took pity on her. "Away with you then, poor child," he said, and he let her go. Then he killed a wild boar, cut out its heart, and took that to the queen.

Alone in the huge forest, the little princess was terrified at every sound. She hurried on, not knowing where she was going.

As evening began to fall, she came upon a little house and, being very tired, thought she might rest there.

Inside, everything was small but very neat and clean. There was a little table covered with a white cloth, set with seven plates and seven knives and forks and also seven little cups. Upstairs stood seven little beds covered with clean white quilts.

Snow White was very hungry and thirsty, so she ate a bit from each plate and drank a bit from each cup so as not to finish up any one portion.

After that, she felt so tired that she lay down on each of the beds. The first was too long, the next too short, another too hard, another too soft; but at last the seventh felt just right, so she lay down on it and fell fast asleep.

When it was quite dark, the masters of the house came home. They were seven dwarfs who mined for gold in the mountain. As soon as they entered, they could see that someone had been in their house, for nothing was as they had left it.

"Who has been sitting in my little chair?" said the first.

"Who has been eating from my little plate?" said the second.

"Who has been nibbling from my little loaf?" said the third.

"Who has been tasting my vegetables?" said the fourth.

"Who has been using my little fork?" said the fifth.

"Who has been cutting with my little knife?" said the sixth.

"Who has been drinking from my little cup?" said the seventh.

Then the first looked at his little bed and cried, "Who has been sleeping in my little bed?" And the others each cried, "Someone has slept in my bed too!"

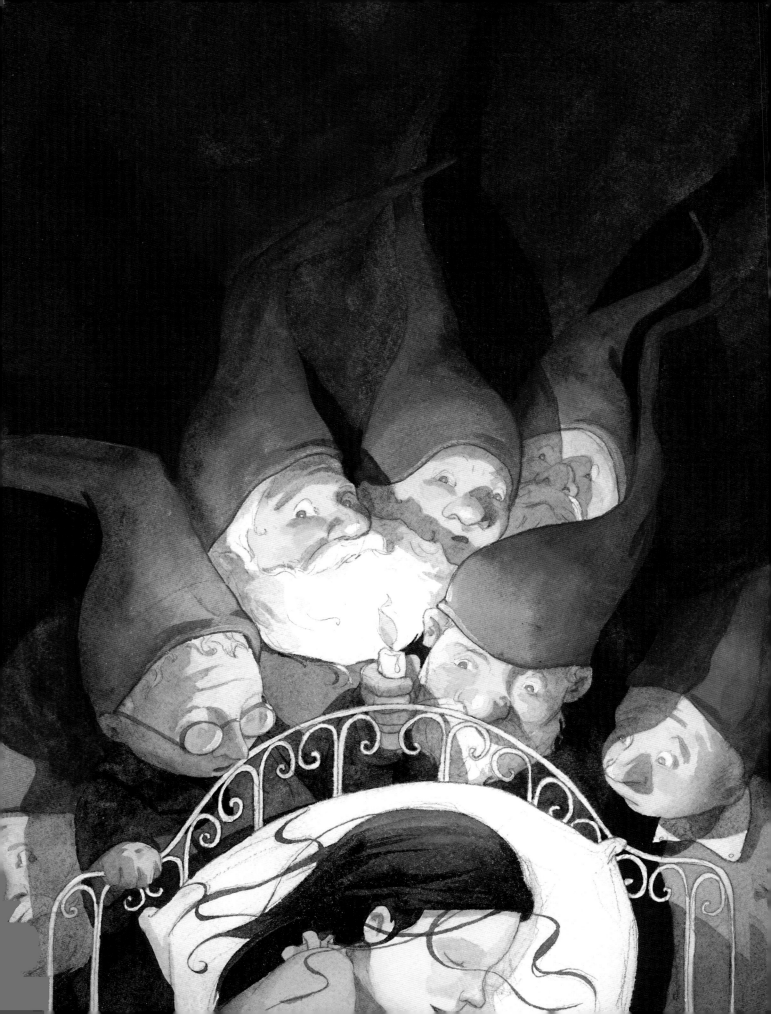

But when the seventh dwarf looked at his bed, there was Snow White, fast asleep.

"What a beautiful child!" cried the dwarfs. And they were so full of joy just looking at her that they did not wake her.

In the morning, when Snow White awoke and saw the seven little men, she was frightened. But they seemed very kind. When they asked her what her name was and how she had come to be in their house, she told them the story of her stepmother and the huntsman.

Then the dwarfs said, "If you will keep our house for us, and cook and sew, you may stay here. But beware of your stepmother. Let no one into the house while we are away."

So Snow White stayed with the seven dwarfs and kept house for them. Each morning she saw them on their way up the mountain to dig for gold. And each evening she had a hot supper ready for them when they came home.

For some time, the queen felt certain that she was the fairest in the land, for she had seen Snow White's heart, had she not? But one day she went to her mirror and said, "Looking glass upon the wall, who is fairest of us all?" And the mirror answered,

> "Queen, thou art of beauty rare,
> But Snow White living in the glen
> With the seven little men
> Is a thousand times more fair."

Snow White still alive? The queen could not bear the thought. As long as she was not the fairest, the queen could not rest for envy. At last she came up with a plan. She dressed herself like an old peddler woman and set off to find Snow White.

When the old woman arrived at the house of the seven dwarfs, she knocked on the door and cried, "Fine wares to sell! Fine wares to sell!"

Snow White peeked out the window. "Good day, good woman," she said. "What have you to sell?"

The old woman held up a bodice lace woven of many colors, so beautiful that Snow White unbarred the door. Surely this old woman could not be any danger, she thought.

"Such a pretty young thing," said the old woman. "Come, let me lace your bodice properly." And Snow White, suspecting nothing, let the old woman lace her bodice.

But the old woman pulled the lace so tightly that Snow White could not breathe, and she fell to the floor as if dead.

"Now, that is an end to you and your beauty!" said the old woman, and she hurried away.

Toward evening, the seven dwarfs came home and found their dear Snow White lying on the ground as if dead. But when they lifted her, they saw how tightly the lace was drawn, and they cut it in two. Then she began to breathe, and little by little the color returned to her cheeks.

When the dwarfs heard what had happened, they said, "That old peddler woman was none other than the wicked queen, your stepmother. You must never again let anyone into the house when we are not here."

No sooner was the wicked queen back in her chamber than she ran to her mirror and said, "Looking glass upon the wall, who is fairest of us all?" And the mirror answered as before,

> "Queen, thou art of beauty rare,
> But Snow White living in the glen
> With the seven little men
> Is a thousand times more fair."

At that, the queen flew into a rage, for she knew that Snow White must still be living. "But now," she vowed, "I will find something that will surely kill her." And with her magic arts, she made a poisoned comb.

Then she dressed herself up to look like another old peddler woman and set off again to the house of the seven dwarfs.

"Good wares to sell! Good wares to sell!" she called.

Snow White opened the window. "Please go away," she said. "I must not let anyone in."

"But surely you are not forbidden to look," said the old woman, and she held up the poisoned comb.

The comb was so pleasing that Snow White could not resist it. Again she opened the door, and the old woman entered.

"Let me comb your beautiful hair," said the old woman. But no sooner did the comb touch Snow White's hair than the poison began to work, and Snow White fell down senseless.

"This time," said the old woman with a satisfied smile, "you are truly dead." And she hurried away.

By good luck, it was almost evening, and the seven dwarfs were on their way home. When they saw Snow White lying on the floor, they knew immediately that it was her wicked stepmother's doing. They looked and found the poisoned comb. Quickly they drew it from Snow White's hair, and she was soon herself again. She told them all that had passed, and once again the dwarfs warned her never to let anyone in at the door.

The queen hurried home and flew to her mirror, demanding, "Looking glass upon the wall, who is fairest of us all?" And once again, the mirror answered,

"Queen, thou art of beauty rare,

But Snow White living in the glen

With the seven little men

Is a thousand times more fair."

When she heard that, the wicked queen shook with anger. "Snow White shall die!" she cried. Then she mixed a deadly brew and made a poisonous apple. It was so beautiful that anyone who looked at it must long for it, but whoever ate even a tiny bite of it would die.

When the apple was ready, the queen painted her face and dressed herself as an old peasant woman. Then she traveled again to the house of the seven dwarfs and knocked on the door.

Snow White opened the window. "I cannot let anyone inside," she said. "I have promised the seven dwarfs I would not."

"That's all right, my dear," said the old peasant woman. "I can easily sell my apples elsewhere. But here, I will give you one."

"No, thank you," said Snow White. "I dare not take it."

"Why ever not?" asked the old woman. "Surely you are not afraid that it is poisoned? Look. I will cut the apple in two pieces. You may have the reddest side, and I will take the other." The wicked woman had prepared the apple so that all of the poison was in the reddest half.

Snow White longed for the apple; and as she could see the peasant woman eating a piece of it, she could not resist. She reached out her hand and took the poisoned half. But no sooner had she taken a small bit into her mouth than she fell dead.

The wicked old woman looked at Snow White and laughed. "This time the dwarfs will not be able to bring you to life again!" she cried.

When she got home, the wicked queen seized her mirror. "Looking glass upon the wall, who is fairest of us all?" At last the mirror answered, "You are the fairest now of all." Finally, finally, *she* was the most beautiful.

When the dwarfs got home that evening, they found Snow White lying on the floor. They looked for something poisonous, but the wicked queen had taken the rest of the apple with her. They cut the lace on Snow White's bodice; they combed her hair. But all was to no avail. Their beautiful Snow White was dead. They laid her on a bier, and all seven of them sat around it and wept for three whole days. They would have buried her then except that she still looked so beautiful. They could not bear to put her in the ground.

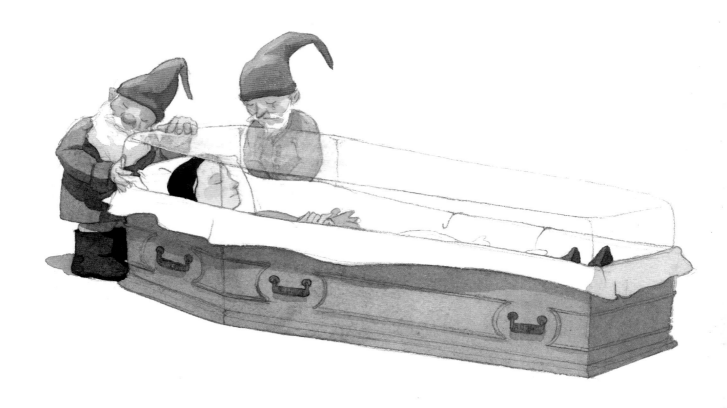

So they made a coffin of glass and laid her in it. On the coffin they wrote, in golden letters, *This is Snow White, Daughter of a King.* They set the coffin in the woods, and one of them always stayed by it to watch.

For a long time, Snow White lay in the coffin and never changed. Her skin was still as white as snow, her lips as red as blood, and her hair as black as ebony. She looked as if she were asleep.

Then one day a king's son rode through the woods and saw the coffin and beautiful Snow White within it. He read the golden letters and said to the dwarfs, "Let me have the coffin and I will pay you handsomely."

But the dwarfs told him that they could not part with Snow White for all the gold in the world.

The prince said, "Then give her to me out of kindness, for I love Snow White more than anything in this world, and I cannot live without looking upon her."

The good little dwarfs took pity on the prince and gave him the coffin.

The prince called to his servants and bid them carry the coffin away on their shoulders. But as they set off, one of them stumbled. The coffin shook; and with the shaking, the bit of apple flew out of Snow White's mouth. She opened her eyes, threw off the glass cover, and sat up, alive and well. "Where am I?" she cried.

"You are near me," the prince answered, full of joy. And he told her all that had happened. Then he said, "I love you more than anything in the world. Come with me to my father's castle and we shall marry."

Their wedding was held with great splendor. Hundreds of guests were invited, and the wicked queen was invited as well. When she had dressed herself in beautiful clothes, she went to her mirror and asked, "Looking glass upon the wall, who is fairest of us all?"

But this time the mirror answered,

> "Though you are of beauty rare
> The bride, my queen, is far more fair."

Then the wicked queen screamed and wailed, and her heart was filled with envy. At first she thought she would not go to the wedding at all, but then she knew that she must see this young bride for herself. When she realized that the bride was Snow White, she was filled with dread.

As punishment for her wicked ways, a pair of red-hot iron shoes were brought forth, and she was made to put them on and dance in them until she fell down dead.

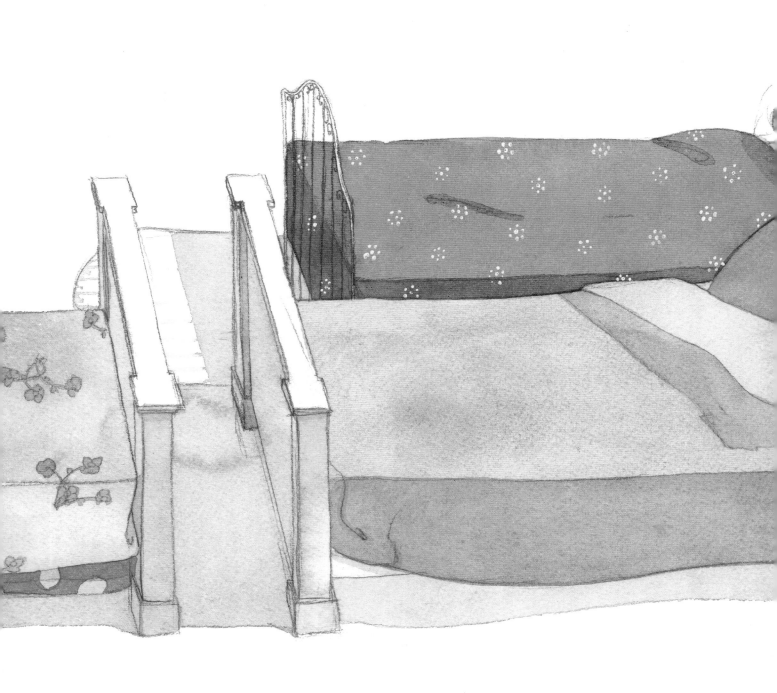